# Happy Birthday, Pirate

For Cap'n Molly and First Mate Max – M.R.
For Adam, who rescues me when I'm all at sea – V.G.

First published in hardback and paperback in Great Britain by HarperCollins *Children's Books* in 2019

1 3 5 7 9 10 8 6 4 2

HB ISBN: 978-0-00-824963-2
PB ISBN: 978-0-00-822712-8

HarperCollins *Children's Books* is a division of HarperCollins *Publishers* Ltd.

Text and illustrations copyright © HarperCollins *Publishers* Ltd 2019

Visit our website at: www.harpercollins.co.uk

Printed in China

MIX
Paper from
responsible sources
FSC™ C007454

FSC
www.fsc.org

This book is produced from independently certified FSC™ paper
to ensure responsible forest management.

For more information visit: www.harpercollins.co.uk/green

# Happy Birthday to you, Pirate

written by
Michelle Robinson

illustrated by
Vicki Gausden

HarperCollins *Children's Books*

Happy birthday to you!

Happy birthday to you!

Happy birthday, dear Pirate.

May your wishes come true!

We've been waiting for you.
Come aboard, join your crew!

Sail forever, search for treasure...

Have a sword fight
or two!

We're the scourge of the sea!

Dance a hornpipe with me …

What a party, me hearty!
Happy birthday to ye!

X is all you can spell.
You don't wash, so you smell!

Your best friend is a parrot...

BOTTOMS!

and a rude one, as well!

There's a patch on your eye.

There's a shark swimming by . . .

There's a haddock in your **hammock** . . .

Are you seasick? AYE AYE!

Let's explore Treasure Bay!

Care to share it...?

No way!

# Happy birthday, dear Pirate!

This is your special day.

Hip, hip, hooray!

Turn the page for a Pirate activity . . .

# MAKE A PIRATE MAP

## Follow the map to find the treasure!

### YOU WILL NEED:

★ A small box or chest, with treasure in it! You can use sweets, small toys, or whatever you would like your crew to find.

★ A large piece of paper

★ Coloured pencils or pens

# How to Make Your Map

⭐ **1** Fill your chest or box with treasure, and hide it somewhere. Don't forget where though!

⭐ **2** Draw a map to your treasure, starting from where you will start to look for it and marking your path with a dotted line.

⭐ **3** Include everything you will need to go past to get there, and mark them on the map. Use your imagination . . .

⭐ **4** X marks the spot! Draw an X at the end of the trail, where the treasure is hidden.

THE GREAT MOUNTAIN

THE DRAGON'S LAIR

THE BLACK LAGOON

THE BIG TREE

TREASURE!

Gather your crew, and go find the treasure!

Bye Bye!